Heal The Hood Foundation Of Memphis
presents

Lil' Red

Story By: LaDell Beamon
Illustrated By: Aaron Liddell

Author Reputation Press LLC
45 Dan Road Suite 5
Canton, MA 02021
www.authorreputationpress.com
Hotline: 1(888) 821-0229
Fax: 1(508) 545-7580

Ordering Information:
Quantity sales. Special discounts are available on quantity purchases by corporations, associations, and others. For details, contact the publisher at the address above.

Printed in the United States of America.

ISBN-13:   Softcover   979-8-88514-099-7
             eBook   979-8-88514-097-3

Library of Congress Control Number: 2022917757

*O*nce Upon A Time in two hoods not too far from you lived Lil Red, the pretty little girl next door in the East and a low down, dice throwing, flesh eating wolf in the North. So the story goes like this, Lil Red was chilling drinking some lemonade hanging with some of her home girls from her social club. This was as friendly as Lil Red got because outside of her family she never socialized. Red was really into her grandmother who stayed in the North, but she rarely saw her because there were rumors about the low down, dice throwing, flesh eating wolf that used to be married to this witch named Gazelle.

3

Everything was going good with Red and her home girls. They were having a great time in Red's sunroom drinking lemonade and eating cheese sandwiches until Red's mom called informing her that her grandmother had come down with the flu. Red loved her grandmother so much until she canceled her get together and struck off to her grandmother's house. Red put on her little red dress, little red pumps and jumped into her little red corvette, and starting bumping Prince's song "Little Red Corvette" on her iPod. Little Red had to make a quick stop at a store to pick up some chicken noodle soup for her grandmother. So she pulled up her GPS to get instructions to the nearest corner store. The GPS pulled up Mom and Pop's Corner store in the South.

On her way into the store, Red bumped into a mysterious hustler who was selling magical cough drops. Red would never speak to people like this guy, but for some reason she decided to buy the cough drops for $20 dollars. She only had $50 bucks, but she gave him a $5 tip. Pops always gave the best advice so he advised Red to get the homemade chicken noodle soup versus the processed soup in the can. She gave him $20 dollars and thanked him and tipped him $5 dollars. Lil Red hopped into her Corvette and didn't notice that the rims were missing and rolled on to the North.

Meanwhile, Wolf had heard about Red's grandmother being sick because he was stalking her on Facebook.

Wolf quickly jogged over to Red's grandmother's house and knocked on the door.

17

Grandma quickly got up from her bed and slowly moved to the door. Without thinking grandma opened the door to find Wolf standing at the door slobbing and smelling like old gym socks. Because of Grandma's bad vision, she couldn't see him very well. She asked who was he, and he said in a raspy voice "Big World a friend of "Lil Red's." She looked at his face and said "What a big nose you have their son". Wolf replied, "I got sinus problems and they swell up sometimes. Grandma said, "Oh that's why your breath smells like that too huh?" "That's why I use Trident gum", replied the Wolf. Red's grandmother focused on Wolf's lips good enough to see these long fangs sticking out his mouth.

19

You got some serious teeth, Big World. Wolf replied, "So I can eat you in two bites." Grandma screamed as Wolf bit her. Wolf's teeth fell out while he was biting Grandma. Grandma laughed as his gums tickled her neck.

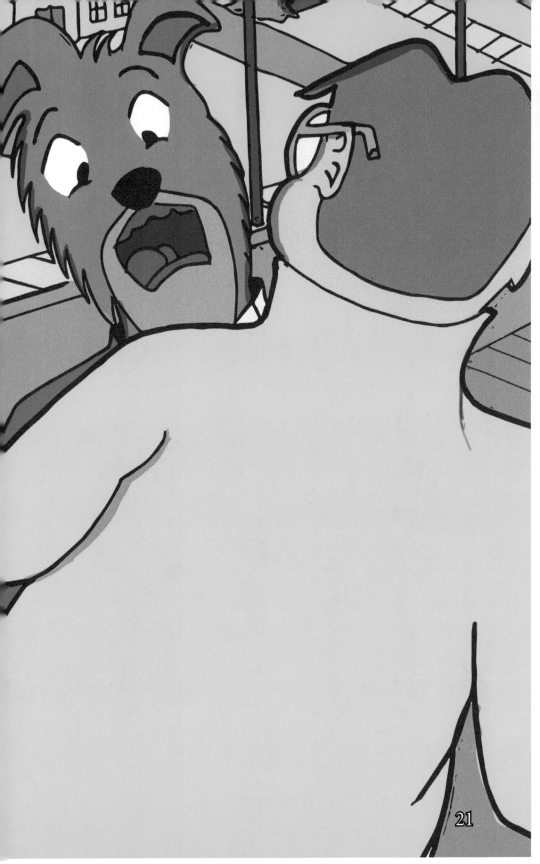

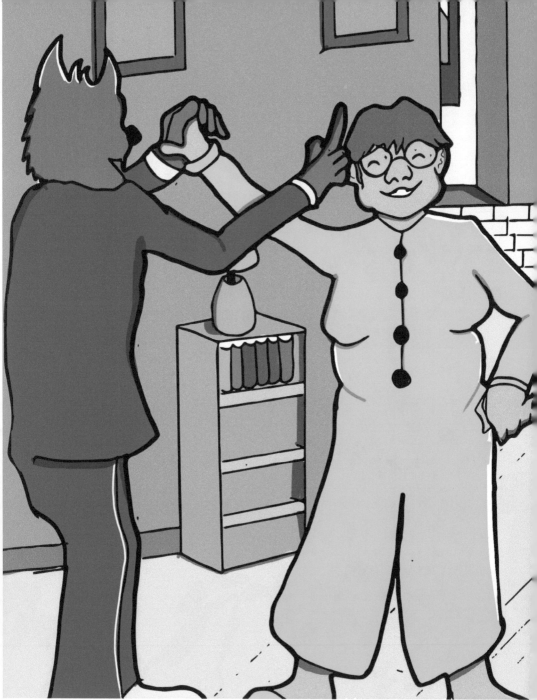

You're so silly Big World; you sure know how to make an old lady feel like a young woman again. Grandma grabbed his hand and said "come here"! As Grandma was trying to get fresh with the Wolf, Lil Red pulled up in the driveway. The Wolf told grandma, "Quick" put me in the closet baby." Grandma told him no, I'll get in the closet you are not rubbing against my clothes smelling like old socks.

Grandma ran in the closet and locked the door. Wolf had no choice but to dress like Grandma and hop in the bed. Lil Red noticed that the door was opened and ran right in with the homemade soup. She closed the door and took the soup to her grandmother's room. When she saw her grandmother in the bed she starting crying, "Grandma, Why is your face so hairy?" Grandma replied, "I haven't been able to cut my hair since I have been sick". Red replied, "And your voice is so raspy. What's up with that foul smell grandma? Wolf replied," I haven't changed my granny diapers".

25

At this point, Grandma heard the Wolf and got upset bursting out of the closet saying I don't wear diapers. Now we have this moment, Red is looking at Grandma, Grandma is looking at the Wolf and somebody needs to start talking. The Wolf says, "Let me explain". I've been following you on Facebook and Twitter. I wanted to show you a real man, but I ended up meeting your grandmother and she got trapped in the closed. "Trapped in the Closet," asked Lil Red. I came all the way over here to take care of my grandmother with this homemade chicken noodle soup and you two have a dating game going on around here. I am so ashamed. From the sound of your raspy voice Wolf, you need this cough drop more than she does. Lil Red gives Wolf the cough drops. As the Wolf takes the cough drops, he magically transforms into Lil Red's grandfather and husband to grandma.

29

Grandma looks at Grandpa and they both look at Lil Red. "We had to do this to get you here, replied grandpa. We all know that Lil Red never goes riding in the hood.

32

THE END

Moral of the Story:

Don't think that you are too good to come down to earth.
Sometimes even the best of us need to be given a reality check even
if it takes a Grandpa in wolves' clothing.

Coming Soon......

Nappylocs and the
Three Bears

CPSIA information can be obtained
at www.ICGtesting.com
Printed in the USA
JSHW071135100523
41503JS00001B/2